AF083579

First published in the UK in 2025 by Studio Press,
an imprint of Bonnier Books UK,
4th Floor, Victoria House, Bloomsbury Square, London WC1B 4DA
Owned by Bonnier Books, Sveavägen 56, Stockholm, Sweden
bonnierbooks.co.uk

© 2025 MARVEL

All rights reserved. No part of this publication may be reproduced or transmitted in any form or by any means, electronic, or mechanical, including photocopying, recording, or by any information storage and retrieval system, without permission in writing from the publisher.

Printed in China
1 3 5 7 9 10 8 6 4 2

ISBN 978-1-83587-043-3

Text: Davide Morando (Arancia Studio)
Artwork & Colour: Jean-Claudio Vinci (Arancia Studio)
Colour: Davide Malantuono, Stefano Porcu, Matteo Tosin (Arancia Studio)
Design: Arancia Studio
Cover design: Alessandro Susin
Production: Giulia Caparrelli

LET'S MEET THE PLAYERS

Loki is looking for a way to escape from Thor's control. To do so, he must travel through time and space to find the pieces of the Light of the Centuries, an ancient artefact that will give him the power to hide from Thor's sight. Meet Loki, Thor, and his allies in these pages – each of them appears somewhere in this book!!

LOKI

Loki is the Asgardian **God of Mischief** and the adopted **son** of Odin, the Father of the Gods. Loki has always lived in the shadow of his brother, Thor, and plots to use his keen **intelligence** and magical skills to seize the **throne of Asgard**!

THOR

Thor is the God of Thunder and the **heir to the throne** of Asgard. He is a brave and fearless **hero** who protects Earth using his enchanted hammer **Mjolnir**. Tales of his legendary deeds are told throughout the universe!

JANE FOSTER

Jane Foster worked for many years as a **doctor** on Earth before being **chosen** by Mjolnir as the new **Goddess of Thunder**. Today, having gained the same **powers** as Thor, she defends Earth and Asgard!

DOCTOR STRANGE

Doctor Stephen Strange was trained in the **Mystic Arts** and became the **Sorcerer Supreme**. With his magic skills, he is the utmost defender of Earth's reality against threats from other dimensions.

CAPTAIN AMERICA

Steve Rogers was injected with an experimental **Super-Soldier Serum** that heightened his strength and agility. He became Captain America, **leader of the Avengers**. He is equipped with a nearly **indestructible shield**!

BLACK WIDOW

Natasha Romanoff was trained to be the Black Widow, a **super-spy** and master of the arts of espionage and **combat**. Now, as a member of the heroic Avengers, Black Widow uses her skills to protect innocent citizens.

AMERICA CHAVEZ

America Chavez has the **natural ability** to use the **energies** flowing between different dimensions to move freely within the **Multiverse**. With her rare skills, she defends the Multiverse!

BLACK PANTHER

King T'Challa is the Black Panther, a sacred title given to the **monarch of Wakanda**, a technologically advanced African nation. His suit is made of **vibranium**, a nearly indestructible metal that can only be found in Wakanda.

OKOYE

General of the **Dora Milaje**, the special forces serving the Wakandan throne, Okoye is one of her nation's **best warriors**, and a **loyal friend** to the Black Panther.

SCARLET WITCH

Wanda Maximoff is a very **powerful sorceress**. Her innate ability allows her to make the impossible possible. This can make her a powerful ally – or a terrible enemy!

SPIDER-MAN

Bitten by a **radioactive spider** as a teenager, **Peter Parker** thwips his webs between Manhattan and the Multiverse as Spider-Man, sowing jokes and serving **justice**!

HULK

Affected by tremendous **gamma radiation**, **Dr. Bruce Banner** became capable of transforming into the incredible Hulk, the Jade Giant. And no one is stronger than the Hulk!

PHOTON

The harbour patrol officer **Monica Rambeau** is one of the most **powerful** members of the Avengers and can **transform** herself into any form of **electromagnetic energy**!

VOLSTAGG, HOGUN, AND FANDRAL

Volstagg the **Voluminous**, Hogun the **Grim**, and Fandral the **Dashing** are the Warriors Three, a trio of Asgardian adventurers. They are **Thor's great friends** and his comrades-in-arms in many exploits across the universe!

BRUNNHILDE

Princess of an **ancient kingdom** conquered by Odin, for centuries she has been **helping the souls** of Asgardians fallen in battle to reach the **paradise of the gods of Asgard**, Valhalla!

KANG

An **evil ruler** who **travels through time** trying to **conquer** Earth and every other planet. He is one of Thor's and the Avengers' **most bitter enemies**. And he has a surprise in store for Loki…

ROYAL LIBRARY OF WAKANDA

Loki must find a way to escape Thor's control. He has found the solution to his problem in an ancient book preserved in the Royal Library of Wakanda: the Light of the Centuries, an artefact that will allow him to travel across time and space without being seen by Thor. Unfortunately, this artefact has been disassembled, and Loki must embark on a journey across many worlds to find the pieces to rebuild it. Can you spot Loki hidden among the Library crowd?

GREAT PYRAMID OF PHARAOH RAMA-TUT

Loki's journey begins at the court of the great Pharaoh Rama-Tut. Here he retrieves the ancient scroll revealing where to find the components of the Light of the Centuries. Now it's time to continue the journey. But where's Loki?

PARLIAMENT OF OLYMPIAN GODS

Loki travels to Omnipotence City, home of the Parliament of Olympian Gods. His mission is to steal one of Zeus's lightning bolts to use as a power source for the Light of the Centuries. Can you spot Loki, hidden among the feasting crowd?

MANHATTAN, NEW YORK CITY

Thor has sent his friends Volstagg, Hogun and Fandral in search of his brother. To escape the gaze of the Warriors Three, Loki chooses to hide in New York City during a battle between the Avengers and the alien Skrulls. Among legions of green alien warriors, who will notice a fugitive Loki dressed in green? You will!

PLANET SAKAAR

On Planet Sakaar, Hulk clashes with other warriors in a gladiatorial contest between champions from many worlds! Swords clash with thunder, scattering sparks, as the Jade Giant shows the audience his fearsome strength. All eyes are on Hulk… so Loki is free to steal the Sakaarian metal he needs for the Light of the Centuries. He must be around here somewhere…

PLANET KREE-LAR

The planet Kree-Lar, home of the Kree Empire, is on the brink of apocalypse! The inhabitants of the capital seek shelter from the devastation as a mysterious starship wreaks terrible destruction on the planet. In all this panic, no one will ever pay attention to Loki, who is haggling somewhere to purchase the parts he needs to build the Light of the Centuries' engine!

JOTUNHEIM, REALM OF THE FROST GIANTS

Having reached Jotunheim, Loki finds himself in the middle of a great battle between the mighty Frost Giants and the warriors of Asgard! Here, in this cold and hostile place, Loki steals the Casket of Ancient Winters, the tool he needs to trigger the Light of the Centuries. Can you spot Loki, sneaking out of the crowd of warriors?

DOCTOR STRANGE'S SANCTUM SANCTORUM, NEW YORK CITY

One of the crystals that must be inserted into the heart of the Light of the Centuries is stored inside Doctor Strange's Sanctum Sanctorum, his home in New York City. The building is now besieged by a spooky inter-dimensional monster, so the main problem for Loki is to find a way to get into the house. But where is he?

AVENGERS MANSION, NEW YORK CITY

Every Saturday, the majestic Avengers Mansion is invaded by tourists who have come from far and wide to see the home of Earth's Mightiest Heroes. The mansion contains not only the trophies of a thousand battles, but also the most advanced Stark technology, essential to assembling the Light of the Centuries! Can you spot Loki among the Avengers fans?

RAINBOW BRIDGE, ASGARD

Surrounded by multiversal waves, Loki tries to cross the Rainbow Bridge which connects Asgard to all the other kingdoms. Hidden among a crowd from every corner of the Multiverse, he draws near to the place where he will finally activate the Light of the Centuries! His journey has almost come to an end! Where is he now?

CHRONOPOLIS, KANG'S CITY

Kang was the mastermind behind everything! Traces of his evil doings are scattered in every part of Loki's journey, and once Loki arrives in Chronopolis to activate his artefact, he must not allow Kang to take possession of the rebuilt Light of the Centuries. Whatever it takes, the Conqueror cannot prevail! It may be difficult to find Loki hidden among the crowd, but if you look hard enough, you will spot him!

TIMES SQUARE, NEW YORK CITY

It's New Year's Eve, and Times Square is packed! With the Light of the Centuries reassembled and activated, Loki is finally able to attend one of the world's most famous street parties – free from his brother's control! Where is he having fun?
Happy New Year to everyone!

FIND ALL THE HIDDEN TARGETS

Our adventure is not over yet! Go back to each location and search for these hidden characters and objects.

ROYAL LIBRARY OF WAKANDA

 Black Panther

 Shuri, T'Challa's sister

 Okoye

 Storm, T'Challa's friend

 Dora Milaje spear

GREAT PYRAMID OF PHARAOH RAMA-TUT

 Khonshu, God of the Moon

 Alligator Loki

 Egyptian symbol

 Golden scarab

 Eye of Horus

PARLIAMENT OF OLYMPIAN GODS

 Hercules

 Ares

 Lord Librarian

 Zeus' lightning bolt

 A cluster of white grapes

MANHATTAN, NEW YORK CITY

 Volstagg

 Hogun

 Fandral

 Nick Fury

 Iron Man's helmet

PLANET SAKAAR

 Hulk

 Grandmaster

 Runa, Brunnhilde's friend

 World Breaker's blade

 Hammer

PLANET KREE-LAR

 Photon

 Vision

 Iron Man

 Kree sentry

 Terrigen crystals

JOTUNHEIM, REALM OF THE FROST GIANTS

 Brunnhilde

 Black Knight

 Throg

 Casket of Ancient Winters

 Destroyer

DOCTOR STRANGE'S SANCTUM SANCTORUM, NEW YORK CITY

 Spider-Man

 Scarlet Witch

 America Chavez

 Doctor Strange

 Darkhold, the book of magic spells

ODIN'S THRONE ROOM, ASGARD

 Thor

 Hela, Queen of Valhalla

 Balder, Thor's best friend

 Mjolnir

 Jane Foster

AVENGERS MANSION, NEW YORK CITY

 Hawkeye

 Captain America

 Black Widow

 Ant-Man's helmet

 Captain America's shield

RAINBOW BRIDGE ASGARD

-  Hulkling
-  Heimdall, sentinel of the Bridge
-  Cosmic Cube
-  Asgardian warrior
-  Ancient amulet

CHRONOPOLIS, KANG'S CITY

-  Iron Lad, a future version of Kang
-  Scarlet Centurion
-  Light of the Centuries
-  Forever Crystal
-  Collar

NEW YORK CITY, TIMES SQUARE

-  Mister Fantastic
-  Thing
-  Human Torch
-  Medusa
-  Seven-League Boots

SOLUTIONS

Loki is circled in red and all the other hidden characters and objects are in white. How good were you at finding each one?

ROYAL LIBRARY OF WAKANDA

GREAT PYRAMID OF PHARAOH RAMA-TUT

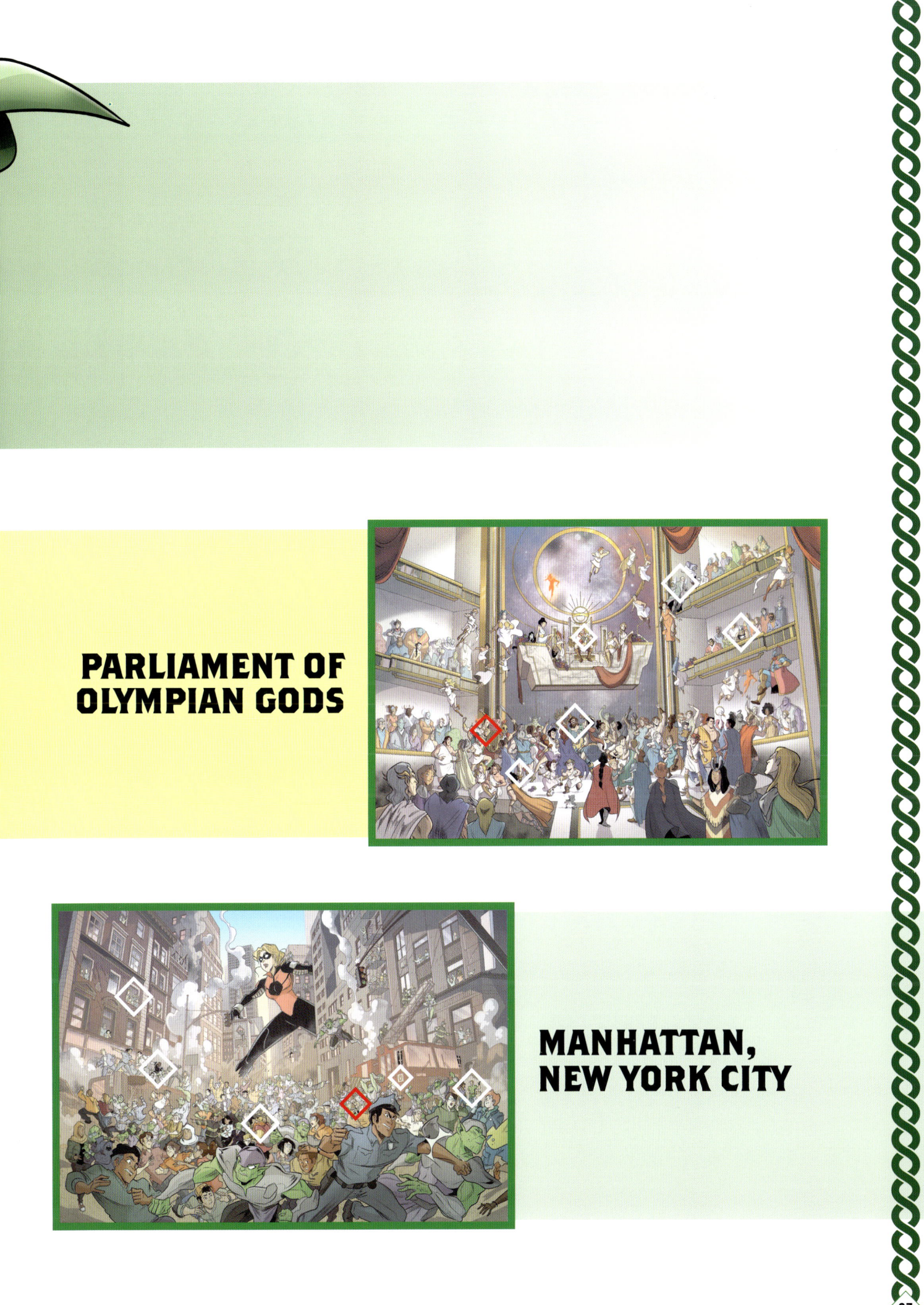

PARLIAMENT OF OLYMPIAN GODS

MANHATTAN, NEW YORK CITY

DOCTOR STRANGE'S SANCTUM SANCTORUM, NEW YORK CITY

ODIN'S THRONE ROOM, ASGARD

AVENGERS MANSION, NEW YORK CITY

RAINBOW BRIDGE, ASGARD

CHRONOPOLIS, KANG'S CITY

NEW YORK CITY, TIMES SQUARE